I Hate Your Guts,
Ben Brooster

I Hate Your Guts, Ben Brooster

Eth Clifford

Houghton Mifflin Company
Boston   1989

Library of Congress Cataloging-in-Publication Data
Clifford, Eth, 1915–
  I hate your guts, Ben Brooster / Eth Clifford.
    p.   cm.
  Summary: When eleven-year-old Charlie's nine-year-old cousin Ben
arrives from Japan with the wrong suitcase to spend a year with him,
Charlie is irritated by Ben's genius intelligence, but comes to
admire him as the two are drawn into a mystery concerning a
handwritten will in Ben's suitcase.
  ISBN 0-395-51079-1
  [1. Mystery and detective stories.   2. Cousins—Fiction.]
I. Title.
PZ7.C62214Iab   1989   89–1863
[Fic]—dc19   CIP
                                                                AC

Printed in the United States of America

P   10   9   8   7   6   5   4   3   2   1

This is for our little golden girl,
Chaya,
who, in her brief life, had the
gift of laughter

Contents

1.
"Why Didn't You Stay Home, Ben Brooster?"

"You're kidding!" Charlie Andrews said. He was so upset he was sure his hair was standing straight up, like the black bristles on his hairbrush. His light gray eyes narrowed as he stared at his mother. "He'll be here *tomorrow?* I thought he wasn't coming until next month."

"Pass the jam," Mrs. Andrews said in a calm voice, as if she hadn't just dropped a hot potato in her eleven-year-old son's lap.

She spread a generous portion of jam on her toast, licked around the edge of the toast to catch the dripping jam, then bit into it carefully. She took a sip of coffee, then explained. "The plans were changed. I got a cable last night. Your cousin Ben is coming from Japan tomorrow to stay with us for a year. Now we've been all over this, Charlie. Ben will have to share your room, as I told you. You can settle between you whether he sleeps in the top bunk or the lower bunk."

Maximilian Andrews, a man with ginger-brown hair that ran down the sides of his face into a beard, gave his son a quick, bright smile.

"Cheer up, Charlie," he said. "This could be the experience of your life." He looked at his watch, finished his coffee quickly, and reminded his wife, "We have to change the window display this morning."

Claire Andrews nodded. She and her husband owned a bookstore sandwiched neatly between a delicatessen and a pizzeria in a busy shopping area. Mr. and Mrs. Andrews changed the book displays often, but they never removed a sign which said: *Your stomach is full*

now. How about some food for thought? READ A
BOOK!

Sometimes Charlie helped at the store, but
today he wasn't interested. He pushed his
cereal around in his bowl moodily, not even
bothering to chase the last few raisins huddled
together at the bottom of the bowl.

He was still annoyed with his father. Great,
he thought. Thanks a lot. That's just what I
need, the experience of my life. What was
wrong with his cousin, anyway? He was probably some kind of weirdo. Why else would his
parents let a nine-year-old travel all that dis-
tance by himself? Aunt Sue and Uncle George
seemed mighty anxious to unload Ben on the
Andrews family.

Maybe it was their fault to begin with. Ben
was two when his parents moved to Japan.
Now he was nine.

"You think Ben is some kind of a nut?"
Charlie asked. "After living in Japan and all?"

Mrs. Andrews sighed. "Well, if he is weird,
maybe you can help straighten him out. That

should be a challenge. You could have avoided all this if you'd taken advantage of Uncle George's offer," she reminded Charlie.

"Yeah. Sure." Charlie stared at the raisins. They looked like small beady eyes staring back at him.

He wouldn't be in this situation if his uncle and aunt, who had good jobs in Japan, hadn't suddenly decided they wanted Ben to get in touch with his own country and its way of life. They had offered to take Charlie in exchange for the year, so he could understand what it was like to live in Japan. But Mr. Andrews felt that Charlie should stay home and help Ben adjust to America.

Secretly, Charlie was delighted with his father's decision. Of course he pretended he wanted to go, but the idea scared him. Stay away from home for a whole year? Go to a country where everybody spoke Japanese, and ate raw fish, and took their shoes off before they stepped inside their houses, and sat cross-legged on the floor while sipping tea from tiny cups without handles?

4

Not Charlie.

He brooded about Ben Brooster as he walked to school. He was so lost in thought that he didn't hear his best friend, Tom Jonas, come up behind him. When Tom put his hand on Charlie's arm to get his attention, Charlie was so startled, he leaped away. Then he glared at Tom, whose red hair flamed in the sunshine, his light brown eyes, usually slitted to shut out the brightness, now wide open with surprise.

"Why'd you go and creep up on me like that?" Charlie demanded.

"I wasn't creeping." Tom was insulted. "I was walking like a normal human being. I'm wearing sneakers. What did you want me to do, go into my war dance or something? What's the matter with you, anyway? You looked like you were a million miles away."

"My cousin Ben Brooster is coming tomorrow." Charlie turned and walked on rapidly. Since he was taller than Tom, he took longer steps. Tom had to hurry to keep up with Charlie's pace.

"*Tomorrow?* He can't do that. We have plans for tomorrow," Tom protested.

"Not anymore, we don't."

"Terrific. I guess that means I can't stay over anymore, either."

Now Tom shared Charlie's gloom. He liked staying overnight. Charlie always let him sleep in the top bunk. The small ladder that led to the bunk was a stairway to adventure. He could pretend all kinds of scary and exciting things. Hanging head down and making goofy faces at Charlie in the lower bunk was fun, too.

Besides, Charlie had the best collection of science fiction stories Tom had ever seen, even better than the one in the library.

Charlie's mother wrote science fiction stories. Some she wrote in a small office at the back of the bookstore, when there were no customers. Others she whipped out in an old closet next to Charlie's room. Mr. Andrews had rebuilt it into a small office, too. It was big enough for a desk, chair, bookcase, a small file, and three wastepaper baskets. Mrs. Andrews claimed the wastepaper baskets were the most important items in the office. She said if she tore up only four pages for every one she kept, she was doing very well.

What Tom especially enjoyed were the evenings Mrs. Andrews would pop into Charlie's room, her glasses pushed up high on her dark brown hair, a faraway look in her deep brown eyes, and say, "Let me try this one on you, okay?"

Charlie didn't mind too much, though he preferred sports stories, but Tom was always fascinated.

"This story is called *The Last of the Martian Gladiators*," she might begin.

Now Tom wouldn't hear any more stories, because Ben Brooster would be taking his space in Charlie's room.

"I hate him," Tom said, savagely kicking a soda pop can someone had dropped on the sidewalk. "I hate his guts."

"*You* hate him? You won't be the one who has to take care of him. A nine-year-old kid. He'll probably be afraid of his own shadow.

He'll probably hang around me night and day."

"Rotten kid," Tom muttered. "Now he's gone and spoiled the last day of school. And tomorrow's Saturday, and I won't even be able to come over, will I?"

Charlie shook his head.

Tomorrow would bring Ben Brooster, and Charlie would be expected to welcome him. Well, if it were up to him, he would look his cousin straight in the eye and say, "Why didn't you stay home, Ben Brooster? Why didn't you just stay home?"

2.
A Day to Remember

"What a perfectly awful day." Mrs. Andrews peered through the kitchen window and frowned.

A strong wind whipped through the trees, tearing at the leaves, forcing the branches to lean heavily to one side.

"Maybe Ben won't be able to come today," Charlie said. He could hope, couldn't he?

"Don't be silly. Of course he'll come. Why wouldn't he?" his mother replied.

Mr. Andrews came into the kitchen, jangling his car keys impatiently. "Let's go."

Charlie glanced up at the clock. "It's way

too early, Dad. We have lots of time. Airplanes are always late. You said so yourself."

"Out!" Mr. Andrews ordered, using his thumb to show his son where the door was.

Mr. Andrews fumed as they slowly made their way through the busy streets on their way to the turnpike.

"Saturday shoppers!" he muttered.

Suddenly a car raced out of the parking lot of a supermarket and smashed into the back of the Andrews car. Mr. Andrews drove forward a little way, turned off the ignition, and leaped out. Charlie was right behind him as the other car came to a stop.

Mr. Andrews yanked the door open on the driver's side of the other car, and demanded, "Are you out of your mind? Who comes out of a parking lot at fifty miles an hour into a busy street . . ."

"Oh, be quiet." A small, heavy woman eased her way out of the car with difficulty. "Don't you dare yell at me. I just hit the accelerator by accident. It could happen to anybody."

10

"Let me see your license," Mr. Andrews said in a cold voice. "If you have one, which I doubt."

At that moment, a gust of wind whipped around the two cars. The woman shrieked, clapping her hand to her head.

"My hair! My hair!"

A curly white wig spun upward, then danced along the street. She began to waddle after it, but it whirled out of reach whenever she tried to grab it.

Charlie stared at her in astonishment. He had never seen a bald lady. Her head was as smooth and as hairless as an egg. And she had glared at Charlie with as much fury as if he had been an Indian on the warpath who had just scalped her.

"Don't just stand there, Charlie. Go get her hair," his father said. "Do you believe this, Claire?" he asked his wife, who had come to join them. "Today of all days?"

Meanwhile, Charlie chased the wig, which looked like a small alien creature without legs making a desperate attempt to escape.

11

Cars driving by hooted their horns when Charlie came too close to them.

At last the wig fell into a puddle. Charlie seized it, holding it out at arm's length. It dripped water as if the creature were crying.

"Yech!" Charlie brought the wig back. "It's wet."

The woman rubbed it with her handkerchief, then plopped it on her head, where it lay like a sick poodle.

"We'll have to call the police," Charlie's mother said. "We're supposed to report an accident."

"Please. Not the cops," the woman begged. "Nobody's hurt, right? Don't call the cops. This is my second accident today. Nothing serious," she added hastily. "It's just not one of my good days. Here." She scribbled her license number on a piece of paper, then added her name, address, and phone number. "Call me tonight, and we'll settle it."

"Settle it tonight? Lady, take a look at the way you bashed my car. You've made a dent so deep in the side, if it was a chair, I could sit in it."

"Max," his wife said. "We're going to be late."

"You shouldn't be allowed on the road," Mr. Andrews roared.

"Please," the woman said, glancing about nervously. "Don't make a scene. I'll pay whatever it costs. Just call me." She held the paper out again.

"Take the paper, Max," Mrs. Andrews urged. "Poor Ben will be terrified if we're not there when he gets off the plane."

When they finally got back into the car, Mr. Andrews sputtered and fumed, and drove as if he were flying a plane. Charlie closed his eyes and decided he'd feel safer up in the air. He was delighted when his feet were on firm ground again.

In the airport, Mr. Andrews consulted an overhead TV screen on which a computer was flashing information. Flight 643 would arrive on time at Gate 27; Flight 921 was delayed and would be an hour late; Flight 220 had arrived early . . .

"Ben's plane came in early? That's ridiculous," Mrs. Andrews exclaimed. "Planes *never* arrive early. I'll just see about this."

She marched over to the ticket counter, past a line of ticket buyers, and rapped for attention.

"There's been a mistake," she told a young man in uniform behind the counter firmly. "Flight 220 wasn't due until . . ." She glanced down at her watch.

"It arrived thirty minutes ago," he interrupted. "Next, please," he said, turning away from her.

"But we are meeting a young child traveling alone," she insisted.

"Just a minute. I'll check." The young man spoke briefly into a phone, nodded a few times, then hung up. "The child is Ben Brooster? Now don't panic," he said in a soothing voice.

"Oh, dear Lord." Mrs. Andrews turned

pale. "Something awful has happened. I feel it in my bones."

"Nothing like that," the young man put in hastily. "He was with a stewardess, waiting at the baggage area, one flight down. She received an emergency telephone call, and just stepped away for a couple of minutes. He promised to stay right where he was, but when she finished the call, he was gone."

"You've lost my nephew? You've *lost* him?" Mrs. Andrews's voice became shrill. "That child must be in a blind panic by now. If anything happens to him . . ."

"No, no, NO!" The young man said instantly, holding up his hand as if to stop her thoughts from racing wildly through her mind. "It's not as bad as you imagine. Our security guards are making a thorough search of the airport. Why, the child may have even returned to the baggage area by now."

"Let's go down there," Mr. Andrews urged. "Ben's a sensible boy, I'm sure. He'd know enough to wait where we would be sure to find him. He probably just got curious and wandered off for a few minutes. You know how boys that age are."

Mrs. Andrews seized on these words with relief. "Of course. Hurry, Max." She began to race toward the down escalator, her husband right behind her.

"Hey. Wait for me," Charlie called.

"Don't you move from this spot," his mother ordered. "Somebody should wait up here, in case Ben comes wandering by. You just keep a sharp lookout, Charlie, you hear?"

Charlie watched his parents run down the stairway to the lower level, too impatient to ride the escalator. Turning away, he glanced about idly and froze. He took a deep breath.

"I don't believe it," he told himself.

A small boy, with straw-white hair and piercing blue eyes, wearing a large backpack, stood alone outside the gift shop. He had a resigned expression on his face, as if he were waiting for someone. He looked just like the snapshot of Ben Mrs. Andrews had shown Charlie.

"Ben!" Charlie shouted as he ran toward the boy. The small boy turned his head and stared at Charlie as he came closer.

"Why didn't you wait at the ticket counter?" Charlie scolded. "My mom and dad are downstairs trying to find you in the baggage area."

In a soft voice, the boy said something Charlie didn't understand.

"None of that Japanese stuff," Charlie commanded. "Not now. Save it for later."

He seized the boy's hand and yanked him along. The boy tried to hold back, but Charlie was much bigger and a whole lot more determined. And so he hauled the boy back to the spot where his parents had told him to wait. His parents were just coming back up the escalator.

"Hey, Mom, Dad," Charlie yelled in triumph. "Look. I found him. I found Ben."

Mrs. Andrews stared at the boy. "You're not Ben." She sounded so angry the boy stepped back. He muttered something rapidly.

"There he goes again, showing off his Japanese." Charlie shook his head.

At that moment, there was a commotion outside the gift shop, followed by the sound of the running of a tall, blond, agitated woman and a stern-faced security officer.

"*Kidnappers,*" the woman screamed as she approached them. "Arrest them!" she ordered the officer.

"Now wait a minute." Mr. Andrews held up his hand. "There has been a slight misunderstanding . . ."

"No misunderstanding. Terrorists, that's what you are." She hit the officer with her handbag. "Don't just stand there. Arrest them!"

The officer rubbed his arm and stood away from the furious woman. "Sir," he began, "this child was forcibly removed from the gift shop by . . ."

"Hoodlum," the woman snapped. "Snake in the grass."

Charlie interrupted indignantly. "I'm no hoodlum. Listen, I thought he was Ben. Why didn't he say something, anyway? In English, so I could understand him?"

"Because he is Swedish. It is only I who have the English, you child snatcher."

It took considerable babble, and embarrassing explanations, and a few more hard blows from her handbag before the woman calmed down. She left with her son, pulling him along by the collar, shouting in his ear.

"I feel positively limp," Mrs. Andrews said. "What do we do now?"

Charlie studied his parents as they stared at each other. Ben had just stepped foot in the United States, and already he was big trouble, Charlie thought. And this was only the beginning! Meanwhile, there still remained this serious problem.

Where was Ben Brooster?

3.
Out Like
a Light

Ben's name was called again and again on the loudspeaker, but there was no reply.

"Go home, Mr. and Mrs. Andrews," the security officer finally told them. "We'll make another thorough search of the airport. We'll check the passenger list again, speak to the cabdrivers. You can't do anything here. Go home, and we'll be in touch with you as soon as we have some news."

The ride home was silent. Mrs. Andrews sat with clenched hands; Charlie huddled in the corner of the back seat; Mr. Andrews stared grimly ahead.

As they turned into their driveway at last,

they spotted a small boy standing near the front steps. Next to him, on the sidewalk, was a large, worn suitcase. Straw-white hair was visible under a cowboy hat tipped well back on his head. Around the crown, letters spelled out the name *Buffalo Bill*. He was twirling a lariat, making a loop that spun around in small circles.

Mrs. Andrews flew out of the car. "Ben!"

The small boy stopped twisting the lariat and waited quietly as she approached him.

"Ben!" she said again, and squashed him against herself in delighted relief. "Ben, you're here."

Ben pushed free. "Of course I am here." He sounded quite matter-of-fact, as if it were only natural that a young boy in a strange land should go to this house like a homing pigeon.

Mr. Andrews shook Ben's hand vigorously. "We had quite a scare at the airport, son."

"I waited," Ben explained calmly. "There was a stewardess waiting with me at first, to make sure someone came for me. Then she got an emergency call. She just talked and

21

talked. I tried to call you, but when there was no answer, I decided something happened and you couldn't meet me. I really didn't need the stewardess. I can take care of myself."

Big shot, Charlie thought. He can take care of himself. What about scaring my mom and dad half out of their minds?

Ben paused, and stared at Charlie, as if he could see Charlie's thoughts. Then he went on, "I asked one of the redcaps to tell the stewardess that I was taking a cab to this address, but I guess he forgot to tell her, since you seem so worried. The airport is so big, I figured it would be best if I came here. After all, I knew you would be coming back sooner or later. It seemed the most reasonable decision to make."

"That was a very sensible, mature decision, Ben." Mr. Andrews nodded in approval.

Sensible? Mature? Charlie stared at his father. What was sensible and mature about not staying put at the airport as he was supposed to?

"He should have waited," Charlie argued.

"Then I wouldn't have grabbed the wrong kid."

"I'm sorry," Ben apologized, though it was clear he wasn't sure why he should be.

"Never *mind*, Charlie! Ben must be starved," Mrs. Andrews said as her husband unlocked the front door. "You scoot on upstairs with Charlie while I get supper ready. You probably want to get out of those clothes after traveling all this time, take a shower or a bath, whatever, Ben. Charlie will give you a hand."

She bustled off to the kitchen as Charlie picked up Ben's suitcase.

Ben gazed up the stairway as if it were Mount Everest and he had to climb it on its worst day.

"You tired?" Charlie asked.

"I'm okay," Ben answered, and reached for his suitcase. "I can carry it."

Charlie looked Ben up and down. He was a head taller than Ben and at least ten pounds heavier. Charlie shook his head.

"If I'm going to have to take care of you,

kid, I might as well start right in. Just follow me upstairs."

As they started up the steps, the doorbell chimed.

"Hello, there, Tom," Charlie heard his father say. "If you're looking for the boys, they just went upstairs."

Tom ran up after Charlie, who guided Ben into his bedroom. "This is my best friend, Tom."

Ben didn't answer.

Charlie put Ben's suitcase on a chair. "You can have the top bunk."

Ben stared straight ahead without expression. Then he leaned against the wall and closed his eyes.

"He's falling asleep standing up. How does he do that?" Tom wondered.

"Don't go to sleep," Charlie exclaimed. "Mom wants us to have supper. Here. I'll help you unpack."

Charlie opened the suitcase and started to lift something out. He turned around and asked Ben, "Are you for real? Who packed this suitcase for you, anyway?"

Ben's eyes opened reluctantly, and his mouth opened even wider. Charlie was holding a long flannel nightgown, with a tiny ruffle of blue lace around the neck and the cuff of each sleeve. A long blue satin ribbon dipped down from string loops on each side.

Charlie threw the nightgown on the floor, reached into the suitcase, and pulled out a blue ruffled satin cap. He rolled his eyes upward. The cap landed on the nightgown.

The next item he took out was a large, boned girdle. The boys had never seen one before.

"What's *that?*" Tom asked.

Charlie held the girdle away from his body as if it had teeth and might attack.

Ben rushed over to push Charlie aside. Then he pulled out one item after another — a plastic cup with a set of false teeth in it, a large-size housedress in a bright blue and red plaid with enormous white buttons that ran down the front, and a white knitted cape Charlie thought at first was a blanket with sleeves.

There were also three pairs of huge, old-fashioned bloomers in an overwhelming pink, a bottle of smelling salts, and a small pillow stuffed with pine needles on which was written in glittering rhinestones:

> Mothers come,
> And mothers go,
> But you
> Go on forever.

Charlie grabbed Ben's hands. "Don't take anything else out. I want to get my mom." He went to the head of the steps and yelled for his mother to drop everything and get right up there.

Mrs. Andrews came tearing out of the kitchen, followed by her husband. They made it up the steps together and burst into Charlie's room.

"What is it?" she panted. "What's wrong?"

Her glance swept the room to settle on the items strewn over the floor. "What in the world . . .?"

Tom Jonas asked, "Is this what kids wear in Japan?"

"Don't be a wise guy, Tom. Can't you see he picked up somebody else's suitcase?" Charlie asked.

"And somewhere," Mr. Andrews explained, "there is a poor old lady sorting through the wrong suitcase, too." He laughed.

"What's so funny?" Mrs. Andrews didn't seem to be amused.

"Poor old soul. She must be wondering what to do with Ben's pants and shirts and socks and shoes."

"I must say this is just what we needed to finish off a perfect day." Mrs. Andrews began to pick the items up from the floor.

While everyone chatted, Ben quietly went to the lower bunk and stretched out. In seconds, he was fast asleep.

"Why don't we just leave all this stuff for

tomorrow? Meanwhile, how about getting some food into Ben. Ben?" she said, looking around.

"He's out like a light. Jet lag." Mr. Andrews covered Ben with a light blanket. "He doesn't need food, Claire. Let him sleep. He'll probably sleep clear through until tomorrow morning."

Charlie's parents left the room, after his mother warned Tom that Charlie would be sitting down to eat any minute.

"I'm leaving," Tom promised. "I just came over to get my baseball mitt."

"You just came to take a look at Ben, you mean," Charlie said when his parents were gone.

The two boys stood silently staring at the sleeping boy.

"So that's him," Tom said, finally.

Charlie frowned. "That's him, all right. And sleeping in *my* bed. If they ever give out awards for top pest of the year, Ben Brooster will get first prize." He shook his head. "I tell you, Tom. This is going to be some year."

4.
"I Can't Talk
on an Empty Stomach"

"I just want to check on Ben," Mrs. Andrews whispered to her son as she followed Charlie upstairs after breakfast the next morning.

"I never saw anybody sleep so hard." Charlie glanced at Ben, who looked as if he hadn't moved a muscle since he fell on the bunk the night before.

Mrs. Andrews picked up the suitcase and started to leave the room with it. "I want to go through this with a fine comb," she told Charlie.

Charlie took the suitcase from her and

placed it on the dresser. "Ben wouldn't hear a volcano erupt in here, Mom."

Mrs. Andrews said, as if to herself, "There just has to be some identification — a letter, or card — *something*. Wouldn't you think someone traveling so far would have a luggage tag? How can people be so careless?" She sounded exasperated, as if the owner of the suitcase should have expected a nine-year-old boy to walk off with it by mistake.

"What do you think you're doing?" she scolded as Charlie dumped the contents of the suitcase on the floor.

"We have a better chance of finding something if the stuff is all spread out," Charlie explained.

"Okay." Mrs. Andrews sank to her knees. She picked up a nightgown and stared at it. "I haven't seen one of these since I visited my grandmother when she was sick." She began to examine the gown carefully. "Listen, Charlie, look in every pocket; turn things inside out to see if anything is pinned on, and . . ."

Charlie interrupted impatiently. "Mom! I'm eleven! I know what to do."

". . . and when you're through," she went on, as if he hadn't spoken, "give each item to me. I'll fold it and put it back. That way, by the time we're finished, everything will be neatly repacked. Now what?" she snapped, as her son picked up the case and tapped it along the top, sides, and bottom.

"I'm listening to see if it sounds hollow. There could be some secret hiding places."

Just then the bell rang, and they could hear Tom's voice. In a moment, he appeared at the bedroom door. Mrs. Andrews ignored him.

"Why in the world would an old lady" — she held up the nightgown and shook it at Charlie in annoyance — "need a suitcase with a false bottom, or whatever?"

Tom whistled. His eyes glittered with excitement. "Is that some special kind of suitcase? You think maybe Ben suspected something and stole it? You think . . ."

"I think," Mrs. Andrews sighed, "you both

should simmer down. We aren't organizing a spy hunt. All we want is some identification, okay?"

Tom leaned down and picked up a garment and held it away. "What's this thing?" he wondered. "It looks like a dress, only it isn't."

"It's called a hoover apron," Mrs. Andrews said in an absent-minded manner, as she ran her fingers up and down the hem of the nightgown.

Charlie grabbed the apron. "It's got pockets. Wait a minute. I've got something!" He waved a long, crumpled sheet of paper in the air.

"Give that here," Mrs. Andrews ordered. She smoothed the crumpled paper, then glared at it in frustration. "Nothing. Just a list of items to take along on a trip. Smelling salts," she read. "Knee warmers. Bunion pads. *The Rise and Fall of the Roman Empire*. Well, at least she's a reader."

Tom had picked up the pillow with the verse on it. "This is a dumb pillow." He sniffed. "But it has kind of a nice piny smell."

32

Charlie's eyes brightened. "Give me that." He turned the pillow round and round. There was no zipper, nor was there an opening that he could see. He was about to toss it aside when he decided to examine it once more. Across the back he found a small, almost invisible ridge he had missed before. He slid a fingernail under the ridge until it popped open. As it did, a long, flat envelope slipped out. He reached for it, but his mother got to it first.

She studied the envelope, then said, "It's a will."

"A will?" Charlie repeated. "But . . ."

Mrs. Andrews held up her hand. "Don't start asking me a lot of questions I can't answer. Just take a look."

She showed the boys the envelope.

In small, cramped letters these words were scrawled: *Last, final, and only will of Barney Bangam.* The envelope was sealed.

"Open it," Charlie cried.

Mrs. Andrews shook her head. "I can't do that. It would be an invasion of privacy."

"This is no time to get technical, Mom. This is an emergency."

Tom agreed. "You can do anything in an emergency. You want me to open it?"

Mrs. Andrews tapped the envelope thoughtfully against the palm of her hand. "Maybe the woman's name is Bangam, too. She could be a relative." Her eyes narrowed. "I think what I'll do first is go through the telephone directory. There can't be too many Bangams listed."

"Suppose she doesn't even live here, Mom. Suppose she's just visiting."

"And suppose her name isn't even Bangam," Tom put in helpfully.

"It isn't," came a voice from behind them.

Three heads swiveled toward the bed, where Ben was sitting up, staring into space. He pressed his fingers against the sides of his forehead. "Grace," he whispered. "It's Grace Aberdeen." He dropped his hands and fell back on the bed.

"Wait!" Mrs. Andrews shouted. "Don't you dare go back to sleep. How do you know her name? Do you know where we can find her?"

Ben opened his eyes briefly. "In a house of many rooms," he whispered again, and fell asleep.

Charlie went to the bed and studied Ben. "Is he one of those psychics? Like some of those nuts . . . I mean, people you write about in your stories, Mom?"

"For heaven's sake, Charlie. The boy is nine years old." Mrs. Andrews's forehead creased in a deep line that pinched her eyebrows together. "A house of many rooms. Does he mean a mansion? I wonder if he was talking about a hotel?"

"Claire," Mr. Andrews said from the doorway. "Is this a private powwow, or can anybody join in?" He pointed to the envelope. "You found something? Mystery solved?" He came closer when she shook her head. Then he, too, examined the envelope. "Did you find anything else? No? Then let's get to the heart of things." Before she could protest, he ripped open the envelope, withdrew a long handwritten sheet, and read it aloud.

Last, final, and only will of Barney Bangam

This is my will, me, Barney Bangam, 95 years old today, January 15th, 1988. Don't let my age bother you because I'm in sound mind (which is more than people half my age can say) and pretty good health, all things considered.

I leave one dollar to my grandson, Bruce Bangam, who thinks money grows on trees. So plant the dollar I'm leaving you, Bruce, and see what comes up.

I leave one dollar to his brother, Bill, who is an even bigger lunkhead.

I bid you both a happy goodbye.

To my niece, Grace Aberdeen, who kept in touch with me over all the long years, who cared for me when I was ill, who listened to all the stories I repeated over and over and never yawned once, who wouldn't touch a penny of my money, I bequeath my house on the old Post Road and everything in it, the grounds and whatever else I own, including a treasure I've hidden.

A clue! It will be right in front of you!

You know me, Grace, and the way I liked to tease you and tell you riddles. So here's a final one for you. Too bad I won't be here when you solve it!

> The flowers that bloom
> in the spring, tra la
> Hide the treasure to
> which they cling, fa la!

This isn't the way a lawyer would draw up this will, but I've lived my life the way I've wanted, and said what I've wanted, and I'm not going to change for anybody at my age.

Written and signed in his own hand by Barney Bangam.

Witnessed by Dr. Mark Change and my postman, Tab Jusin.

"Wow!" Charlie said.

"This can't be for real." Mr. Andrews studied the paper and shook his head. "The old boy must really have been somebody to write home about."

"A secret treasure. Boy! Am I glad I came over today," Tom said.

"This still doesn't help us. Who is this Grace Aberdeen? And *where* is she? What are you up to now?" Mrs. Andrews called after Charlie, who was racing from the room.

"Downstairs. To see if she's in the telephone book. If she isn't, I'm going to call every hotel in town."

"I'll help." Tom ran after him.

Mr. Andrews shrugged, then glanced over toward the bed. "Well! Look who's come back to life. Hi, Ben. Welcome back."

Mrs. Andrews turned. Ben was sitting up, definitely wide awake, and smiling.

"How did you know that woman's name even before the envelope was opened?" she asked, somewhat sharply.

Ben's smile broadened. He opened his mouth.

Both Mr. and Mrs. Andrews waited, expectantly.

Then Ben said, "I can't talk on an empty stomach. When do we eat?"

5.
Something Fishy
Is Going On

"I found her!" Charlie burst into the kitchen where Ben was eating pancakes and sipping orange juice. He waved a paper in the air. "She's at the Drake Street Hotel. Room 321."

Mr. Andrews ran his hand across Charlie's head affectionately. "Charlie Andrews, boy wonder detective."

Mrs. Andrews snatched the paper, dialed the number Charlie had written down, asked for Room 321, and then turned on the speaker phone so everyone could hear the conversation.

A woman's voice came on. She didn't say hello. Instead she shouted angrily, "You're not scaring me, you birdbrain, whoever you are. I'm calling the police."

"Mrs. Aberdeen?" Mrs. Andrews asked uncertainly. "Is this Grace Aberdeen?"

"So there's a woman in this little scheme of yours, whatever that is? Now I *am* calling the police."

The receiver was banged down hard.

Mrs. Andrews stared at the phone, then at her husband. "What in the world was that all about?"

"Maybe she's just a certified nut," Tom suggested. "My dad says there are a lot of kookie people running around these days."

Ben stopped eating. He seemed offended by Tom's remark. "She happens to be a well-educated, interesting, fine lady, with a clear, sharp mind."

Charlie glared at Ben. "Oh, yeah? How do you know? Are you still pulling that psychic stuff on us?"

"Yes, Ben. How *do* you know?" Mr. Andrews reached out to stop Ben's hand in midair just as he was about to pop another bit of pancake into his mouth.

Ben gave him a teasing smile. "Maybe I am psychic."

Mr. Andrews tapped his fingers rapidly on the table. "And maybe we're getting a little impatient, Ben. We'd also like the explanation you've been putting off. How did you know Mrs. Aberdeen's name before we even opened the envelope?"

Ben put his fork down. "She was sitting next to me on the flight here. Most of the passengers were small Japanese women. Since Mrs. Aberdeen was the tallest lady on the plane, I figured the nightgown had to be hers. Just a little deductive reasoning on my part, that's all. I'm not really psychic." Ben winked at Charlie. "And I know she's well-educated because she's a teacher. I found her interesting because she told me so many stories about her travels. She really does have a clear, sharp mind."

Mrs. Andrews frowned. "And she is also

one very frightened old lady. I wonder why."

"Call her again, Claire. See if you can get a word in edgewise before she . . ."

Mrs. Andrews had already begun to dial before her husband finished speaking. As soon as she heard Grace Aberdeen's voice, she said rapidly, "This is Claire Andrews. Please listen to me. You sat next to Ben Brooster on the plane."

Everyone in the room could hear Mrs. Aberdeen's deep sigh of relief. "Thank heaven," she said.

"Is something wrong?" Mr. Andrews joined in the conversation. "Has someone been threatening you?"

"It's these phone calls I've been getting. Someone whispering, warning me to get out of town. It's been very upsetting. And I didn't know how to get in touch with you about my suitcase because there is no identification in the one I accidentally picked up, and I couldn't remember the name of the family Ben would be staying with, and . . ."

Mrs. Andrews interrupted. "Would you

like us to bring your suitcase to the hotel?"

There was a pause. "I'd rather come to your house, if you don't mind. I do need to talk to someone."

"No problem," Mr. Andrews said at once. "I could drive over and pick you up right now if you like."

There was another long pause. "No. I need to rest. I'm still weary from the flight. Can I come after lunch, say about two o'clock? I'll take a cab."

"Poor old soul," Mrs. Andrews said as the phone clicked off.

"It's mighty mysterious, isn't it?" Tom was delighted.

Charlie shook his head. Tom not only loved science fiction stories; he was also an avid reader of mystery books as well, the scarier the better. Charlie could tell Tom was ready to shoot off in all directions. He was the one who'd like to be the boy wonder detective.

Mrs. Andrews looked up at the clock, then at the breakfast dishes, which were still on the table and counter.

"Clean up, boys," she ordered. She didn't see why she should prepare all the meals and then have to clear up afterward as well. "Dad and I are going to the store for a while," she told Charlie. "We'll be back in plenty of time."

Charlie wasn't surprised. His parents always checked in at the store briefly on Sundays, although Mrs. Senter took over for the day, and had for years.

While Charlie and Tom cleaned up the kitchen, Ben wandered into the living room. When the boys were done, they found Ben sitting almost lost in Mr. Andrews's favorite chair, a section of the newspaper folded, regarding the page thoughtfully, pen in hand.

"Hey!" Charlie yelled. "What do you think you're doing?" He moved closer to Ben and stared down in disbelief. "Do you know what you've done? My dad waits all week for the *New York Times* Sunday crossword puzzle, and now you've gone and scribbled all over it. *In ink!*"

He didn't explain that his father always used

a pencil, so he could erase his wrong answers.

"Don't yell at him, Charlie. He's just bored, right, Ben?" Tom sounded understanding and patient. "Just like my kid brother, Andy. He's nine. He'll be in third grade when school opens. He could bring some games over. He's got a terrific Tinkertoy . . ."

Ben was outraged. "You want *me* to play with a Tinkertoy? ME? With a third-grader?" He turned furiously to Charlie. "For your information, I wasn't scribbling. I was *doing* the puzzle. In fact, I had just finished when you came in."

Before Charlie could reply, Tom said, still patient but surprised at Ben's reaction, "You don't understand, Ben. Just sticking letters in any old way isn't . . ."

"Spare me," Ben interrupted. He turned to Charlie. "Didn't your parents tell you about me?"

Charlie shrugged. "What's to tell?" Except, he thought rebelliously, that I had this feeling about you all along. Trouble, that's what you are. Big trouble.

"I'm a genius."

Tom fell to the floor and pounded it as he roared with laughter.

Charlie, however, didn't even smile. "Okay. So you like to kid around. First you're a psychic, and now you're a genius. Great. So you get some good marks in school. Terrific. Now I'll tell you something, Ben Brooster. I'm a straight A student, but I don't go around telling people I'm a genius."

Ben sighed. "You're going into sixth grade when school opens in the fall, right? You, too, Tom?" When they nodded, he said, "I'll be entering the final year of junior high."

Charlie was furious, and didn't know why this sudden rush of anger was so overwhelming.

"Prove it, wise guy," he shouted.

Ben stared at him. "What do you want me to do? Talk to you in a foreign language? Okay. Pick one. I speak Japanese and English, of course. I also am fluent in French. I know a bit of Russian, and I have a smattering of German. I expect to enter college by the time I'm eleven. I plan to be an astrophysicist. Any other questions?"

"An astrophysicist?" Tom repeated. "I can't even spell it."

"So what? Big deal. I'm going to be a brain surgeon," Charlie yelled, and stormed out of the room. "Why am I so mad?" he asked himself. He opened the door of the refrigerator and stared blankly at the food on the shelves. Whenever he was angry or upset, he became hungry. While he studied the various items, he muttered to himself, "A world full of nine-year-old kids, and this one has to be Superkid."

"Are we going to have a snack?" Tom, who had followed Charlie into the kitchen, joined him at the refrigerator. He could eat dessert at any time of the day, and the chocolate-iced cake looked especially inviting.

"I'm hungry, too. I missed supper last night, you know." Ben spoke from the doorway. His hat was back on his head; the lariat was now looped on his right arm.

That irritated Charlie. What was with this

kid and his obsession with a *Buffalo Bill* hat and a rope that was like an attached third arm?

"You expecting to lasso a wild bull or something?" Charlie asked.

"If there was one here, I would." Ben gave Charlie a defiant look. "You want to see exactly how I would do it? Just watch."

Ben concentrated, squinting his eyes as if he were on a dusty road with the sun blazing overhead, staring at some invisible object coming toward him.

"Yippee-ai-ay," he shouted suddenly. Before the boys realized what had happened, Ben had lassoed one of the kitchen chairs.

"Hey! You're really something," Tom said with admiration.

Charlie wouldn't admit he was surprised. "Terrific. You captured a dangerous chair."

Ben ignored Charlie. Turning to Tom, he said, "I can lasso anything. I'd probably be even better if I was on a horse."

"Do you ride?" It wouldn't have startled Tom. This kid probably could do anything he put his mind to. "I wish I had a horse," he went on, without waiting for Ben's answer. "That's one thing Charlie and I always wanted, right, Charlie?"

"Do you guys ride?" Ben asked.

"That's like asking if Buffalo Bill was a cowboy," Charlie replied with scorn. Noticing that Tom was about to speak, Charlie frowned him into silence. "How come you're so interested in horses, and lassoing chairs, and wearing a cowboy hat? What do they know about cowboys in Japan anyway?"

"Westerns," Ben said, with frost in his voice, "are the most popular shows on television in Japan."

"Sure." Charlie didn't believe Ben. "Like their favorite sport is baseball, right?"

"Yes. Baseball is a favorite sport in Japan."

"Baseball is an American game." Charlie shouted.

"It's a Japanese game," Ben shouted back.

Tom glanced from Ben to Charlie and back again. "Come on, guys," he urged. "We came in here to eat, remember?"

"I'm so hungry I could eat a bear." Ben

tried to sound the way he thought a tough Westerner out on the range might speak.

"We're fresh out of bear," Charlie said. "But there's some raw fish in here. Why don't you make a meal out of that? It's brain food, you know. Or maybe you think you've got so many brains you don't need any more."

"I'll eat it if you will," Ben replied.

"I can do anything you can do." Charlie removed the dish from the refrigerator, holding it well away to avoid the fishy odor. Raw fish! His stomach curled in knots at the idea.

Ben looked in the refrigerator and found a lemon, a bottle of oil, and a shaker of mixed seasonings. While the boys watched, he prepared a dressing, then poured it generously over the fish, after which he divided the fish into two precise portions.

"Any time you're ready," he told Charlie politely.

Tom watched in fascinated disgust as Ben dug in, licking his lips after each small bite. Charlie, feeling green inside and out, took one tentative bite and swallowed. He could feel his eyes bulging out of his head, but he pressed his lips together to force the fish down. He choked and clapped his hand to his mouth. Perspiration broke out on his forehead. His nostrils flared out.

He rose from the table so quickly his chair fell over. Without looking back, he fled to the bathroom.

As soon as he was gone, Ben tore over to the kitchen sink and threw up.

"Yech!" Tom said, moving well back into the room.

When Ben could talk, Tom said, "I thought people in Japan like raw fish."

"Not me," Ben gasped. "I hate the stuff."

"Then why'd you eat it?" Tom asked with surprise. "Listen, my brother Andy isn't too bright, but he'd be smart enough not to eat something he can't stand."

"Charlie made me mad," Ben admitted. "I guess we were both rather childish."

They could hear the TV from the living room. Charlie had bypassed the kitchen to avoid Ben.

51

"I'm going to take off," Tom said. "If you ever get to talking to Charlie again, will you tell him I'll be back at two o'clock?"

Ben nodded. However, when he peered into the living room, the sight of Charlie, arms folded, staring at the TV with a stony expression, put him off. He decided to go upstairs, where he fell wearily into the lower bunk.

Suddenly he felt lost and sad. He longed to be home again. Nothing had gone right since he'd come to America.

Tears ran down his cheeks. "This is ridiculous," he said aloud. "Geniuses don't cry." He thought about that for a moment. "But I'm still only nine years old. I guess I can be a kid."

And so he cried himself to sleep.

6.
Tweedledum
and Tweedledee

"Hello. We're home," Mrs. Andrews shouted, as she and her husband came rushing in a little before one o'clock. "Charlie! Ben! A treat for lunch. Kentucky fried chicken, cole slaw, fries, and Cokes."

"That figures." Charlie came into the kitchen to help set the table. Once a week his mother made the same announcement, and somehow always sounded as if she expected her trip to a fast-food place to be a welcome surprise.

"It's better than eating home cooking," his father said, and winked at Charlie. That was no surprise, either. His father made that same remark week in and week out.

"Where's Ben?" Mrs. Andrews asked.

"How should I know?" Charlie had cooled off somewhat since his encounter with Ben earlier, but it had left him feeling out-of-sorts.

"He's a guest in our house," his mother told him sharply. "And your responsibility as well as ours. Why don't you know where he is?"

A guest? Was his mother serious? Ben would be living with them for one whole year. That was no guest. That was cruel and inhuman punishment.

"Probably asleep," Mr. Andrews guessed. "It takes a while to adjust. I think I'll get my crossword puzzle. I can get a start on it before we eat."

"Wait a minute, Dad." Charlie didn't want to tattle, but he felt his father ought to be prepared for what he would find. "About the puzzle . . . I don't think you should bother with it today."

"I know. I know. Mrs. Aberdeen will be

here at two. I don't expect to finish it, Charlie. Not in an hour, anyway."

Charlie shook his head. "It's done."

Mr. Andrews was startled. "What do you mean, done?"

From the doorway, Ben said in a subdued voice, "It's my fault. I did it, Uncle Max."

For a brief moment, Mr. Andrews looked angry. Then he forced a smile. "Why, that's all right, Ben. Don't give it another thought. I am curious, though. How long did it take you?"

"Ten minutes," Ben said, sounding apologetic.

"Ten minutes," Mr. Andrews repeated. He no longer looked angry, just depressed.

"Never *mind*." Mrs. Andrews looked at her watch and then at the clock on the wall. "We've got to eat fast. I imagine Mrs. Aberdeen is the kind of person who always arrives exactly on time."

Mrs. Andrews was right. Just as the grandfather clock in the hall chimed twice, the doorbell rang. Waiting on the doorstep was a tall, husky woman clutching a suitcase. Her thin hair, cut in wispy bangs across her forehead, was gray. Her eyebrows, impossibly black, had been penciled in an arch over each eye, giving her a permanent expression of surprise. Her hazel-brown eyes were framed by rimless glasses pinched onto the bridge of her thin nose. She wore a dress that appeared to have been cut down from a tent.

"Mrs. Andrews?" she asked. Her voice, which had been a little shrill on the phone, was like soft music. That was how Mrs. Andrews described it to everyone later.

"Come in. Come in," Mrs. Andrews urged.

"Me, too." Tom stepped out from behind Mrs. Aberdeen.

Ben, who had followed Mrs. Andrews to the door, bowed, then said joyously, "Mrs. Aberdeen!"

Charlie, hearing that joy in Ben's voice, thought uncomfortably, Why, he's greeting her just as if she's the only friend he has in the world. For a moment, Charlie felt sorry he'd made his dislike for Ben so obvious. Then Ben spoiled it by adding, "Welcome to this humble house. You honor it with your presence."

"Humble?" Charlie repeated with outrage. "What do you mean, 'humble'?"

Ben ignored Charlie. He led Mrs. Aberdeen directly to Mr. Andrews's chair, which was the most comfortable one in the room. "Please deign to sit in this miserable chair," Ben told her.

Mrs. Aberdeen caught the expression on Charlie's face. "It is the Japanese way of speaking to a guest," she explained. She turned to Ben, who was trying to put a pillow at her back.

"I'm fine, Ben." She took a deep breath. "Well, not really. I have been most upset by the phone calls."

"Maybe they were just crank calls," Mrs. Andrews suggested. "That does happen, you know. People calling numbers at random."

"Oh, no, my dear. Whoever it was had to seek me out, get my room number, ask to be put through. Oh, no," Mrs. Aberdeen said again. "The person on the phone meant to call me. He was most insistent. 'Get out of town. NOW!' he told me."

"I'll bet it was the two Bangam brothers," Ben said. When Mrs. Aberdeen stared at him in surprise, he added, "They were mentioned in the will. Barney Bangam's will."

"You know about the will?"

Mr. Andrews put in hastily, "We weren't prying. It was the only way we could think of, opening the will and reading it, to find out who the suitcase belonged to. I'm sorry."

"Please." Mrs. Aberdeen held up her hand. "It's understandable. I think Ben is right. The voice on the phone was disguised, but it probably was Bruce Bangam." She sighed. "I don't like it, but it does help to put a name to a voice, doesn't it?"

"Is he dead? Your uncle, I mean," Tom asked.

Mrs. Aberdeen's eyes were sad. "Yes. It's why I took leave from the school where I teach in Japan. I did it once before, when Uncle Barney was ill. About five years ago. He was kind of a feisty man." She smiled, remembering her uncle. "His neighbors used to drop in on him from time to time. They didn't mind his peppery ways. They were used to him. While he was in bed," she went on, still remembering days gone by, "I read horror stories to him." She shuddered. "They were awful, but Uncle Barney loved them. When he could get out of bed, we went to see every horror film for miles around."

Charlie's eyes gleamed. Even more than sports stories, he enjoyed horror movies, real scary, goose-pimply, screamy, spine-chilling horror movies. "Boy, that must have been fun," he said with envy. His mother put her foot down when it came to Charlie's choice of movies.

"They're usually rather stupid, I think," Ben said, "and quite juvenile for the most part."

If Charlie's glare had been a sword, it would have run Ben through and pinned him to his chair.

"And not really frightening, once you realize

how they are made," Ben continued, giving Charlie a mean little smile. He was still angry.

Not really frightening? Charlie thought. I'll fix you, Ben Brooster. Wait till you go to sleep tonight. I'll put on that Godzilla outfit I wore to the Halloween party last year. Then I'll climb up the ladder to the top bunk and howl in your ear. Maybe I'll sneak Tom over . . . we'll see who isn't scared all right.

He beamed at Ben, startling him.

Meanwhile, Tom explained to Mrs. Aberdeen, "I've been thinking. Ben is absolutely right. It's got to be the Bangam brothers who called."

When everyone turned to look at him, Tom added, "I read mysteries all the time. And in a book, the Bangam brothers would be prime suspects." Tom leaned forward and said to Ben, "Prime means . . . oh, I forgot." He put his hand over his mouth for a minute. "See, I always have to explain a new word to my brother Andy."

"I'm sure," Ben muttered, scowling.

"I'm certain now it was Tweedledum and Tweedledee." Mrs. Aberdeen laughed. "That's what Uncle Barney called them, when he wasn't calling them lunkheads."

"Because they're short and round and always together?" Ben asked, smiling.

"And dress as if they're twins, though they aren't. And both have bald, round heads," Mrs. Aberdeen added.

"This is all very interesting, and mysterious, but I don't quite see what we can do to help you," Mr. Andrews said.

"I was hoping you could go with me to my uncle's home. I'm really rather afraid to go there alone since the phone calls came. Bruce did sound very threatening."

"Yes, of course," Mr. Andrews replied politely.

"And we could look for the treasure! Please, Dad," Charlie pleaded. "Can't I come with you?"

Mr. Andrews turned to find three pairs of eyes fixed on him hopefully. "Tell you what, boys," he told them. "We'll make it a Sunday outing."

"Wait," Ben said. "I have to get my hat. And my lariat." He dashed out of the room. Mrs. Aberdeen smiled fondly after him, but Charlie shook his head and rolled his eyes heavenward.

"While we're waiting" — Mrs. Andrews couldn't control her curiosity — "do you mind if I ask you why you hid your copy of the will in that . . ."

". . . awful pillow," Mrs. Aberdeen finished for her as Mrs. Andrews stopped speaking abruptly.

"I know. It was a Mother's Day gift," Charlie said.

Mrs. Andrews frowned at her son, which made Charlie wonder what she would do if he ever bought her a pillow like that.

"No, Charlie. I have no children. I bought it myself. I'm so absent-minded these days. I put things down and then can't find them. Since I travel a lot, I worried I might lose something important. I just use the pillow as a forget-me-not reminder. I've kept money in it, my passport, the copy of the will when Uncle Barney sent it to me." She waved her hand. "And I can leave it on my bed wherever I go. After all, who would steal a pillow like that?"

Just then, Ben came bouncing down the steps, his hat firmly jammed on his head, his lariat in position on his arm.

"Feel better now?" Charlie's voice had a sarcastic edge to it.

"Yes. I do. This is my good luck hat. And you never know when a lariat will come in handy."

Charlie nudged Tom and laughed. "And he's supposed to be a genius."

Tom turned to study Ben. His eyes were thoughtful as he replied, "I don't know, Charlie. This kid is full of surprises."

7.
The Flowers That Bloom in the Spring, Tra La

"It's a long drive," Mrs. Aberdeen warned as she settled between Tom and Ben in the back seat of the Andrews's station wagon. Because she was so big, Charlie had to sit up front between his parents.

Charlie turned to say something to Tom, but waited in surprise as Mrs. Aberdeen broke into rapid speech. "Hey! Is that Japanese you're talking?" he asked.

"This is a *private* conversation, and yes, it's in Japanese. So do you mind?" Ben snapped.

"Well, where's this Japanese politeness Mrs. Aberdeen was telling us about before we left the house? I don't think it's very good manners to talk about us in a language we don't know."

"We're not talking about you, Charlie," Mrs. Aberdeen explained. "In fact, we're talking about Ben. I told him I know that he must be terribly homesick. And sad. After all, he won't see his home or his parents again for a full year."

"Oh." Charlie hadn't thought of that. Was he being too hard on Ben? Because he suddenly felt guilty, he told himself, I don't care. He's a smart alec and I don't like him.

"I will miss the Boys' Festival," Ben said, as if talking to himself.

"What's that?" Tom asked. "It sounds like fun."

"Every house in which there is a son flies a streamer shaped like a carp. The streamers are attached to long poles in the gardens or on the roofs."

"A *carp?*" Charlie repeated. "A *fish?*"

"It is very colorful and exciting," Mrs. Aberdeen put in quickly when she saw the angry look in Ben's eyes. "The carp is considered a very brave fish, for it swims against even the strongest current. The carp is a sign of strength and courage."

"And I will miss the National Poetry contest," Ben said, with a catch in his voice.

"Poetry? You write poetry?" Tom wondered. "You *like* it?"

Again Mrs. Aberdeen came to Ben's rescue.

"Nearly everyone in Japan writes poetry. It is a country that loves the beauty of words, and of flowers, too."

"So? Big deal," Charlie muttered. "We have plenty of flowers in America, you know."

"He doesn't understand. I don't see why you had to tell him anything." Ben sat back, folded his arms, and looked glum. "Whose side are you on, anyway?"

"Why, Ben. I'm not taking sides. I just think you cousins might get along better if you knew something about each other's feelings." Mrs. Aberdeen seemed upset. Once again, she added a few words in Japanese.

Ben answered her in English. "I wish I had

never come. At least at home everyone was used to me. Now I suppose I'll have to live through this whole business all over again. Why do kids automatically hate me when they find out I'm a genius?"

"They think it's a reflection on them somehow." This time Mrs. Aberdeen spoke in English, too. "And of course they're jealous. Surely you're used to that?"

"I am not jealous," Charlie insisted immediately. He sounded insulted. But he couldn't help thinking, I am jealous. I hate having a nine-year-old kid smarter than I am. It *bothers* me.

As if she could read Charlie's thoughts, Mrs. Aberdeen said, "You know, Charlie, Ben can't help it if he's smarter than . . ." She stopped abruptly. Her hand flew up to her lips. Then she sighed, "Oh, dear, I'd better stop talking. I'm making things worse."

"I'm not jealous, either," Tom said. He laughed. "Just think of all the help I'll be able to get from you. I could go from a C student to an A student, like Charlie. Maybe some of your genius will rub off on me. Wouldn't that be something?"

"You see, Ben?" Mrs. Andrews smiled. "You're among friends here. Right, Charlie? Right, Charlie?" she repeated, when her son didn't answer immediately.

"Sure." Charlie stared at Ben. "No problem."

Ben stared back. "Terrific," he said.

Mrs. Aberdeen stared out the window, then cried out happily, "Look. We're passing the Crosscreek Riding Stable. Uncle Barney and I used to see some wonderful horse shows there. He rode a lot in his younger years, but I never could bring myself to get up on a horse. I guess I never saw a horse I was sure could move once I got on." She grinned. "I think it would take two of them to carry me."

"I love horses," Tom said. He gazed at the horses wistfully. "But I only got to ride a pony once."

"Me, too," Charlie agreed. "Ponies are nice when you're real little, but I sure would love to get on a real horse. What about you, Ben?"

Maybe, Charlie thought, he could practice being nice to Ben once in a while.

Ben shrugged. "I guess I could ride as well as anyone, if I ever got the chance."

"We should take a drive out this way more often," Mrs. Andrews commented. "The countryside is quite beautiful."

"There seem to be many more houses here now," Mrs. Aberdeen mourned. "Oh, well. It's to be expected, I suppose. Everywhere you go, change after change. Nothing stays the way you remember it. Except," she added, pointing out the window, "al's eats. Uncle Barney used to come to that diner for breakfast, when he was strong enough to walk to it from the farmhouse."

"You mean we're almost there?" Tom was relieved. He hated long car rides. He didn't get carsick often anymore, but the feeling seemed to lurk in his stomach, ready to pounce at any time.

"Oh, yes, Tom. As a matter of fact, we turn into this road just past the diner."

Mr. Andrews drove carefully, for the road was rough and filled with potholes. It led to a large gray farmhouse with a sagging porch. The house had a forlorn and neglected look, with bare windows like sightless eyes.

Mrs. Aberdeen sighed. "It used to be such a beautiful place. I imagine Uncle Barney was too old to care these last few years. Good heavens!" she gasped, as the car moved closer to the house. "What's happened here?"

Mr. Andrews stopped the car. Everyone piled out to stare at plants that lay uprooted all around them. Blossoms lay twisted and torn, roots exposed, wilting in the hot sun.

"Somebody's been after the treasure," Charlie said. "What a mess!"

"Somebody who knew the clue in the will," Tom added. "Remember? The flowers that bloom in the spring, tra la?"

Mrs. Aberdeen began to run toward the back of the house, for she had heard voices. The others followed swiftly behind her. They came to an abrupt halt at the sight which greeted them. A large area of the backyard, which was a meadow gone wild, had been dug up ruthlessly. Two men stood resting on their shovels, quarreling in loud, angry voices, their round perspiring faces red with exertion, their chests heaving.

"The Bangam brothers?" Mr. Andrews asked.

"I can't believe it," his wife said. "They really do look like Tweedledum and Tweedledee."

They reminded Charlie of weighted toys he had once had that bounced back into position when they were tilted.

"BRUCE BANGAM! BILL BANGAM! If you're not off these premises in two minutes, I'll call the sheriff." The expression on Mrs. Aberdeen's face told them she meant what she said.

The two men glowered at her, then raised their shovels to their shoulders. They marched toward their car, which they had parked in a small space at the back of the house.

"You're not blood kin. You were only married to his nephew," Bruce Bangam shouted at her spitefully.

"So by rights the treasure is ours. And you can't tell us any different," Bill Bangam added.

"Why don't we let the sheriff decide?" There was acid in Mrs. Aberdeen's voice.

Bill Bangam threw the shovels into the trunk, slammed the lid shut, and followed his brother into the car.

"You've not heard the last of us," he shouted out the window as they drove off.

"Well," Mr. Andrews said, trying to bring a little cheer to their faces. "Why so grim, everybody? Look at it this way. They've sure saved us a lot of digging."

"A good thing, too," Charlie agreed as he glanced about. "It could take a week to dig under every flower back here."

At the sound of an approaching car, Mrs. Andrews spun around. "Not the brothers again! Even they wouldn't have the nerve to . . ."

She broke off at the sight of the man who stepped out of the car. He was tall and straight as a steel rod. Though the sun was high and merciless in the sky, he wore a jacket buttoned tightly and a tie knotted firmly in the collar of his stiff shirt. A small breeze had sprung up, but his black hair remained unruffled, as if glued to his head. His glasses were black-rimmed and heavy and exactly matched his expression.

"He's got to be the funeral director," Mr. Andrews muttered, "come to ask Mrs. Aberdeen to pay the funeral expenses."

But the man, who introduced himself as John Joseph Tranquil, was the banker from the Third Federal Savings and Loan in the nearby town, who had come seeking Mrs. Aberdeen.

"But how did you know I was here? And why have you come looking for me?" Mrs. Aberdeen was puzzled.

"When I couldn't find you at your hotel, I felt it was my duty to see if you were here. I've come to tell you what I told the Bangam brothers. Just two weeks before his death, Barney Bangam withdrew every last cent from his account at our bank. To the tune of $165,418. In cash."

Tom and Charlie stared at him wide-eyed. Ben frowned. Mrs. Aberdeen gasped. Mr. and Mrs. Andrews were speechless.

"He just walked in, carrying a large metal box with a small padlock on it, told me it was stainless steel, couldn't rust, was waterproof, and would I just kindly fill it up."

"Why didn't you stop him?" Mr. Andrews wondered. "Surely an old man like that . . ."

"He was just begging to be robbed," Mrs. Andrews interrupted. "Where was your common sense?"

"Madam." John Joseph Tranquil's voice was so cold it could have frozen boiling water. "Can you force a waterfall to flow upward? Can you insist a cow bleat like a goat? I couldn't talk him out of it. He kept saying it was going to be his last joke. A riddle, if you please."

"Did he tell you he was going to bury the

box under one of the plants in his garden?"
Charlie asked.

"Young man. He chuckled his way in, and
guffawed his way out. Said the Bangam brothers wouldn't find it if you rubbed their noses in
it, but his niece Grace would catch on."

Mrs. Aberdeen looked pleased, but consid-
erably puzzled.

As a parting shot, John Joseph Tranquil
said, "He did emphasize that the box was
waterproof and rustproof. Draw your own con-
clusions. I washed my hands of him then. I
wash my hands of him now."

With that, John Joseph Tranquil turned
away, got into his car without another word,
and drove angrily away.

Mr. Andrews gazed at the flowers that still
bloomed, and sighed. "I guess we start
digging."

"With what?" Tom asked.

"Yeah, Dad. We never thought to bring any
tools," Charlie pointed out.

Mrs. Aberdeen said, rather absent-mindedly, "Uncle Barney kept all his garden tools in the basement." She shook her head. "Poor Mr. Tranquil. It must have driven him wild to see all that money leaving."

She led the way to the back door, which was unlocked. "Uncle Barney didn't believe in keys. He said if someone was bound and determined to get in, he would, and there wasn't anything to steal anyway. What a contradictory old man he was."

Mr. Andrews tried the switch in the kitchen. "The electricity is off. Can you find us some candles, Mrs. Aberdeen?"

"Yes, of course." Mrs. Aberdeen found candles and some long wooden matches in a tin box over the stove.

"Charlie. You and Tom come down with me," Mr. Andrews said. "We'll bring up whatever useful tools we can find. We'll be back up in a few minutes."

The two women sat down in the kitchen. Ben climbed up on the counter and twirled his lariat thoughtfully, his eyes hidden by his cowboy hat.

Mr. Andrews led the way down the narrow steep stairway, his candle held high. Charlie and Tom followed with their own candles.

The women could hear them as they walked carefully down the steps and stumbled their way into the basement.

Then, suddenly, there was no sound at all. The women looked at each other uneasily. The silence seemed unnatural.

Then came the thud of someone falling, a terrified shout, and a high-pitched scream that sent icy chills up and down their spines.

8.
A Nice Place
for a Nightmare

Ben leaped down from the counter, looped his lariat over his left arm, lit a candle, and sped to the basement door. The two women also lit candles and followed Ben down the narrow stairway.

"What is it?" Mrs. Andrews called out as she clutched the railing on her way down. "What's going on?"

"Did somebody get hurt?" Mrs. Aberdeen shouted.

No one answered.

When Ben reached the last step, he paused to peer into the darkness. Why weren't any candles glowing? Ben hugged his lariat against his body. Whoever was down there wouldn't get away, not if Ben could help it. He would hogtie the intruder. He was sure that was the right expression — hogtie.

Mrs. Andrews brushed by Ben impatiently. "Max? Charlie? Where are you?"

"Over here," Charlie called to his mother.

The two women and Ben walked hesitantly into the basement. Now, with the aid of their candles, they could see a little further into the darkness.

Mr. Andrews sat on the floor, holding his head. Tom was a silent sprawled figure on the floor. Charlie stood next to them, trying to relight his candle with a shaking hand.

Mrs. Andrews ran to her husband's side. "You're hurt. Max! You're bleeding!"

Mrs. Aberdeen pushed his hand gently aside. "Well, it's not bad at all. Your skin is scraped." She whipped a large handkerchief from the pocket of her dress and wound it neatly around Mr. Andrews's forehead.

"I hit it on something when I fell, and I bumped into Tom and knocked him down. I think he hit his head. I can't be sure," he said.

Ben stared at Tom's body. "Is he dead?"

"He just passed out, I think." Charlie shuddered. "I almost did myself."

Mrs. Andrews turned to speak to her son, stiffened, then filled the air with a piercing shriek.

Charlie nodded sympathetically. "I know, Mom. I screamed, too, when I saw those . . . those freaky things in the corner."

Mrs. Aberdeen sighed. "Oh. Those figures, you mean. Thank goodness, child. I thought something really terrible had happened down here."

"Something terrible did happen." Charlie had been so scared, he hadn't had time to be angry. Now he was furious. "Who keeps *monsters* in his basement?"

Tom sat up and rubbed the back of his head. "What happened?" he whispered. "Last thing I recall, Mr. Andrews knocked me right off my feet. Oh! I remember. Those weird creatures. Are they still there?" he asked faintly, unwilling to look.

Mrs. Aberdeen could see an explanation was needed. "I'd forgotten all about these figures. Uncle Barney had a wax museum for years and years. He called it Barney Bangam's Hall of Horrors. When he retired and closed the museum, he had the figures shipped here. He just couldn't bring himself to part with them."

"They look so real, I could have sworn they were moving," Mr. Andrews admitted. "That's when I backed up and fell."

In the candlelight, the wax figures were ominous. A man, his face twisted with hatred, held a knife in the air. The look in his eyes was chilling. Nearby, Dracula bared his fangs as he spread his black cloak like the wings of a bat. Godzilla's mouth was wide open with a silent roar that could almost be heard. A werewolf howled up at an invisible moon.

Tom was still somewhat shaky. He nudged Charlie. "You still like horror stuff, after all this?"

"Now that I know they're only wax, I don't mind," Charlie said. "It was just coming across them in the dark like that."

While the others studied the figures, Mrs. Aberdeen found two lanterns hanging on a wall. She lit both and handed one to Mr. Andrews. Then she said, "Over here. I want to show you something."

Everyone crowded around her. Charlie's eyes glowed with delight. One long wall was covered with huge posters. At the head of each poster large black letters, with red paint dripping from them like blood, proclaimed:

BARNEY BANGAM'S
HALL OF HORRORS

Beneath these words was a slogan: *A Nice Place for a Nightmare.* The letters in the word "nightmare" seemed to shimmer and shake.

Enormous figures filled each poster. Under the figures, the monsters were identified.

See Godzilla Destroy Tokyo
See Dracula in His Coffin
See the Werewolf Howling at the Moon
See Frankenstein's Monster Come Alive
See Jack the Ripper in Action

"I saw Jack the Ripper in action." Charlie took a deep breath. "I bumped into something, looked up, and there was this maniac with his knife coming down right at me. That's when I screamed," he admitted.

"Which startled me, so I tripped and fell," Mr. Andrews said.

"And knocked me out cold," Tom added.

"I think I for one would never set foot down here." Mrs. Andrews was emphatic. "They're monstrosities. Do you plan to keep them?"

Mrs. Aberdeen's answer was prompt. "Not I. I never did like them. Since I plan to go back to Japan, I have no use for them anyway. I'll have to get rid of them somehow."

"Why not give them to Uncle Max?" Ben asked.

"Me?" Mr. Andrews asked with surprise. "What would I do with them?"

"I'm assuming you have horror books in your store. If you were to set off a corner," Ben explained, "put up a few of these posters, set up a different figure or two every month, you'd have a real conversation piece. I bet that would bring more customers into the store, even if they only come to look at the display."

Mr. Andrews's eyes grew thoughtful. His head began to nod. "What a fantastic idea. Claire, we could clear out the storage area and turn it into 'The Corner of Horrors.' If Mrs. Aberdeen will let me buy the whole shooting match."

"Buy? Not on your life," she replied at once. When his face fell, she added firmly, "Give them to you, Mr. Andrews. Take everything here, with my blessing."

Mrs. Andrews didn't seem too pleased. Her husband persuaded her. "Claire, just think of the publicity. Maybe we could expand on the idea later, after we see how this works out. You know. Have a science fiction corner?"

"You don't have to hold that out as bait," she replied, smiling. "I know a good sales promotion when I hear it." She tapped her teeth with a finger in a rapid little motion, a sign she was thinking. "What are we going to do about those posters? They all have Barney Bangam's name on them."

"Keep them just as they are. I think they'd add punch to the idea," he told her.

"How Uncle Barney would have loved that." Mrs. Aberdeen beamed. Impulsively, she caught Ben up in her arms. "You're a genius, Ben. A genuine, all-around genius."

"I know," Ben said. He gave his lariat an expert twirl.

"I'd have thought of that if I hadn't been taken off guard by Jack the Ripper," Charlie muttered.

"He wouldn't have frightened me. I'd have lassoed him where he stood," Ben bragged.

"Why don't you go soak your head, stupid?" Charlie whispered in Ben's ear.

Not waiting to see Ben's reaction, Charlie turned to his mother. "Aren't we forgetting what we came down here for? We still have flowers to dig up in the garden, remember?"

"Charlie! Of course! The flowers!" Mrs. Andrews hugged him. "Seems to me we have two geniuses in our midst."

Charlie sent Ben a triumphant look.

"Can we talk about this upstairs?" Tom

pleaded. "I don't care if these figures are only wax. They give me the willies."

"I agree," Ben said. "They do still appear to be moving. I know it's just a trick of the shadows, but I'm going back upstairs."

Without waiting for a reply, Ben shot up the steps.

"I'm with him," Tom agreed and made his way to the narrow stairway.

Mr. Andrews looked around. "I see some garden tools in that corner. Charlie, give me a hand. Claire, you take one of the spades."

Once they had sorted out the tools they needed, they climbed slowly up the steps and into the kitchen.

"I've been thinking— " Ben began when they were all together again.

"So have I," Mrs. Aberdeen interrupted. "It's not been a pleasant afternoon, has it? I suggest, since it is so hot, that we postpone the digging until tomorrow."

"What I'm trying to say," Ben tried to get their attention, but Mrs. Andrews sighed and said quickly, "I agree. Let's come back very early tomorrow morning, when we're fresh. I for one am not getting out under that broiling sun to dig, treasure or no treasure. No, Charlie," she added firmly, as he began to protest. "The treasure will keep."

"Suits me." Tom was relieved. "I've had enough excitement for one day."

Ben seemed frustrated. "I went into the living room — " he tried again.

"Terrific. They'll announce it on the six o'clock news." Charlie was impatient now that the treasure hunt had been postponed. "I'm starved. Can we stop off on the way home for a pizza?"

"All in favor, say aye," Mrs. Andrews said.

Everyone but Ben shouted hearty ayes.

"Was there something on your mind?" Mrs. Aberdeen asked Ben, when they were all back in the car and on their way to the pizza parlor.

"It doesn't matter. It can wait till tomorrow." Ben tipped his cowboy hat down over his eyes, looped his lariat on his arm, and whispered to himself, "Who listens to a nine-year-old kid anyway?"

Charlie's hearing was sharp. He leaned over and whispered back, grinning, "Nobody. And don't you forget it."

9.
Barney Bangam's
Last Laugh

"Seven A.M.," Mrs. Aberdeen announced as she looked at her watch. "I do like getting out early in the morning like this." She beamed. "Riding through the countryside this way. Everything so peaceful and serene."

"Max and I feel just as if we're playing hooky," Mrs. Andrews said. "Taking a Monday off and not going into the store. This is going to be an absolutely perfect day. I just know it."

Charlie felt so good he didn't mind the least bit today that Ben had his hat on and his lariat looped around his arm, as usual.

"Today's the day we find all that money,"

Charlie said, his eyes shining with anticipation.

"It's not our treasure," Tom reminded him. "It belongs to Mrs. Aberdeen."

"Who cares?" Charlie drew a deep breath. "It's a treasure, isn't it? I never found a treasure before in my whole life."

"I found a quarter in the street once," Tom remembered. "My mom said it was dirty and to let it lie there. But I picked it up anyway."

"I had an idea yesterday," Ben began eagerly, but Mrs. Andrews interrupted.

"I feel just as excited as I am when I attend a Trekkie convention."

"Mom means she's a Star Trek fan. She collects Trekkie stuff." Charlie broke off to stare at Ben. "I don't suppose you know what I'm talking about."

Ben stared back, then replied coldly, "We're quite progressive in Japan. We even know what television is, believe it or not."

"I know what you mean, Claire," Mr. Andrews agreed with his wife. "I have the same feeling. I could almost be going to another Crossword Puzzle Competition."

When Charlie opened his mouth to explain, Ben held up his hand. "Don't tell me. Let me figure that out all by myself."

Charlie was silent. You couldn't tell Superkid anything. He knew it all. It didn't matter, though. Today was the day, and nothing was going to spoil it.

Somehow the ride seemed shorter this morning. True, Mr. Andrews drove too fast on the highway and faster than he should on the country road. The sight of AL'S EATS diner was a welcome reminder that the journey was almost over.

"Shall we stop and have coffee?" Mrs. Andrews asked somewhat wistfully. What she really wanted was breakfast — scrambled eggs, bacon, and lots·of home fries, because she had had only one cup of coffee this morning and a slice of slightly burned toast.

Mr. Andrews shook his head and drove on. "Later," he said. "Maybe."

Almost before the station wagon came to a stop in front of the Bangam farmhouse, the doors were swung open and everyone jumped out.

"I left the tools in the kitchen," Mr. Andrews started to say, when Mrs. Aberdeen clutched his arm.

"Oh no!" She was furious. "Do you hear what I hear?"

The sound of spades hitting dry, hard ground carried clearly in the morning quiet.

"I guess they've just taken up where they left off yesterday." Mrs. Andrews looked upset.

"They said you hadn't heard the last of them," Charlie reminded Mrs. Aberdeen.

"How dare they!" she exclaimed. "How dare they come back!"

The Bangam brothers had surely arrived at dawn's first early light, for flowers were strewn everywhere. Bushes in bloom lay, roots exposed. Gaping holes showed how deeply the brothers had dug.

The brothers were digging doggedly again,

unaware that they now had company. Just as Mrs. Aberdeen was about to shout at them, the clang of metal striking metal rang out.

"We found it!" Bill Bangam's voice was loudly triumphant. "We found it!" He danced wildly around his brother.

"Dance later," Bruce Bangam commanded. "Help me get the box up."

They cleared space around the box, lifted it out carefully, then brushed the dirt off the box, finally polishing it off with their arms.

"We're rich! We're rich! We're rich!" Bruce Bangam chanted.

"Bruce Bangam. Bill Bangam. You bring that box here. On the double!" Mrs. Aberdeen could have been a general giving orders to her troops.

For a moment, the Bangam brothers were so startled, they almost obeyed her command. Bill started forward, then stopped. Bruce hugged the box close.

"We've got to stop them, Max," Mrs. Andrews said.

Mr. Andrews nodded, looked around for a

likely weapon, and picked up a broom leaning against the kitchen wall.

Tom whispered to him, "That diner isn't too far. I could run back there in less than ten minutes. If you can keep them here till then, I can get the sheriff on the phone."

"Good boy. Go to it," Mr. Andrews told him.

Meanwhile, the Bangam brothers watched Mr. Andrews warily.

"We don't want any trouble," Bruce Bangam warned finally. "We only want what's ours by right. So move out of the way, all of you, and we'll get in our car."

"Give us the box and you're free to leave," Mr. Andrews said.

Bill waved his shovel threateningly. "You let us pass or I'll brain you."

Mr. Andrews took a few steps closer to the brothers. Charlie went to stand beside his father. As he did so, he noticed Ben edging away from them.

"That's right, Superkid. Find a safe place

for yourself." Charlie's voice was filled with contempt.

Ben ignored him. He continued to edge away, till he stood completely clear off to the side. Concentrating on circling his lariat in ever-widening circles, he kept his eyes on the Bangams, who were so intent on Mr. Andrews and his broomstick they were unaware of Ben.

Suddenly, Ben let the loop of the lariat fly. It made a zinging noise as it whipped through the air. When the brothers, startled, looked up, Bill dropped his shovel and turned to run.

The whirling loop caught and held them as Ben tugged desperately at the other end of the rope.

"Wow!" Charlie said. He was stunned. It had happened so quickly, he had almost missed seeing the lasso flying toward the brothers.

"Help me," Ben gasped, as he yanked on the lariat.

Mr. Andrews dropped the broomstick to leap to Ben's aid. His strong arms finished what Ben had begun. The brothers were securely caught. The more they struggled, the tighter the loop became. Pulling them close was like yanking an obstinate, fighting fish out of water.

"Let's get them into the kitchen," Mrs. Aberdeen said.

Still struggling, and shouting threats, the brothers were finally pushed into the kitchen and tied to two chairs.

Charlie had picked up the box, which had fallen to the ground when the brothers had been lassoed. "Can we open it?" he asked eagerly, holding the box out to Mrs. Aberdeen.

"Give it to your father. You'll have to smash the lock open," she told Mr. Andrews.

He nodded, put the box on the floor, and brought his foot down hard. The small lock flew open. He then placed the box on the table, bowed to Mrs. Aberdeen, and said, "Madam. Will you do the honors?"

The Bangam brothers leaned forward anxiously.

Mrs. Aberdeen stretched out her hand, let her fingers rest on the box, then pulled her hand away.

"I don't think I can." Her voice sounded suddenly faint. "Anyway, I think Ben should open it. After all, he captured our would-be thieves."

"Please. Somebody. Anybody. Open it," Bruce Bangam begged hoarsely.

Charlie felt disappointed that Mrs. Aberdeen had chosen Ben, but he had to admit to himself that Ben deserved the honor.

At that moment, the kitchen door flung open, and Tom rushed in, with the sheriff close on his heels.

The sheriff was a bear of a man, tall, heavy, with long arms and large hairy hands. He was red-faced from too much sun. When he removed his hat to mop his forehead, his hair sprang upward in a mop of bristly black curls.

"'How did you get here so fast?" Mr. Andrews wondered.

"The sheriff was having breakfast when I got to the diner," Tom explained.

"That's no big surprise." The sheriff's voice was big and loud. "I have breakfast there every morning at this time. Another two minutes and the boy would have missed me. I gave him a lift back in my car. He filled me in on what these two have been up to, so I'll just take them off your hands. You pressing charges, Mrs. Aberdeen?"

She was pleased. "You remember me, Sheriff?"

"Yes, ma'am. You took care of your uncle. I looked in on him from time to time, you know." He jerked his finger at the Bangams. "I can hold them for vandalism, trespassing, stealing . . ."

"We never even got a chance to steal anything," Bruce Bangam yelled. "They've got the box and the fortune. It isn't fair. We did all the hard work."

"Up you go." The sheriff reached out to pull the Bangams to their feet.

"You can't take us now. Not until somebody opens the box. At least we should get to *see* the money," Bill Bangam protested.

As the sheriff shrugged, Ben opened the box. There was a gasp of surprise from everyone.

"It's empty!" Bruce Bangam said in a strangled voice. "That old fox! He's diddled us out of a fortune."

"Not empty altogether." Mr. Andrews reached into the box and removed a bright red plastic fish. "There's this."

Mrs. Aberdeen giggled. "Uncle Barney and his jokes."

Bill Bangam didn't think it was funny. He was outraged. "What does it mean? Why would he put a plastic fish in the box?"

"It's a herring," Tom said, and grinned. "Don't you see? It's a red herring."

"I'm not colorblind. I know red when I see it," Bruce Bangam roared.

"Yeah, Tom." Charlie was puzzled. "What's the big deal about a red herring?"

"You should read mysteries instead of horror stories." Tom sounded smug. "A red herring is a false clue. Mystery writers do that all the time. They throw in false clues so you won't

99

guess right away who the guilty person is."

Ben had pulled the box closer and examined it while Tom was explaining. Now he said, "There's a piece of paper in here, too." He picked up a small sheet with a verse written on it, which he read aloud.

> The flowers that bloom
> in the garden, ha ha
> Have nothing to do
> with the case!

Mrs. Aberdeen was amused. "Uncle Barney's last laugh."

The sheriff, who had untied the Bangam brothers meanwhile, firmly marched them out of the kitchen. They were still protesting. "It's not fair. It's not fair." The words floated back to the kitchen.

"I'll tell you what isn't fair," Mrs. Andrews said. "It isn't fair to have raised your hopes this way and then play you for a fool. Barney Bangam may have had the last laugh, but you're out a fortune."

"Oh, my dear, somehow I could never quite

believe in the treasure, anyway." Mrs. Aberdeen sounded wistful.

"Is that it?" Charlie looked as gloomy as he felt.

"We were robbed," Tom said.

"We might as well take off." Mr. Andrews was clearly upset.

"No. Wait." Ben smiled at them. "There is still a treasure to be found, believe me. And I think I know exactly where it is."

10.
You Don't Have to
Be a Genius

A pang of such deep envy shot through Charlie, it made him wince. Ben, with his straw-white hair and blue eyes, his cowboy hat fixed firmly on his head, the lariat back on his arm, looked exactly like a third-grader. He was such a *little* kid. Why did he have to have a giant brain? At that moment, Charlie sincerely and heartily wished an ill wind would blow Ben back to Japan.

"I just hate his guts," Charlie muttered to Tom. Tom, however, like the others, had been stunned into silence. But, disregarding Charlie, he was now the first to speak finally.

"Where is it? Where, Ben? Come on. Just don't stand there."

Ben wasn't in a hurry to tell. He liked the effect his announcement had on all of them. When Mr. Andrews's foot began to tap impatiently, Ben asked, "Doesn't anybody remember what Barney Bangam said in his will?"

Charlie waved this aside with irritation. "He said a lot of things."

Mrs. Aberdeen put in helpfully, "The flowers that bloom in the spring, et cetera?" She knew Ben was enjoying his big moment; she didn't mind a bit.

"No." Mr. Andrews was thoughtful. "It was something else."

"I remember, Max," his wife said. "Wasn't it, 'It will be right in front of you'? That was one of the clues, wasn't it?"

Ben nodded approvingly.

"But all those flowers *were* right in front of us," Charlie argued. "We were even going to dig them up, except that Tweedledee and Tweedledum beat us to it."

"I tried and tried to tell you yesterday," Ben reminded them, "but nobody would listen."

"We're listening now, dear boy."

That was true enough. Every eye was fixed on Ben.

"Then come into the living room with me."

Everyone followed Ben obediently. They walked into the middle of the room and waited.

"Look around," Ben instructed them. "What do you see?"

They studied the walls, the floor, the ceiling, the furniture. What was it Ben expected them to see? Then a great light flashed on in Charlie's mind.

"The wallpaper," he cried.

Flowers bloomed on all the walls. Pink and lavender blossoms, with endless small green leaves, climbed trellises from floor to ceiling.

"The flowers that bloom in the spring, tra la, hide the treasure to which they cling, fa la," Mr. Andrews recited. "Of course. The wallpaper! What do you say, Mrs. Aberdeen? Do we let it rip?"

"Be my guest. Please."

Never had wallpaper been stripped from walls with more enthusiasm and excitement. The boys ripped up from the bottom; the adults stood on chairs and ripped down from the top. Some of the money had to be peeled off where it had stuck to the wallpaper. But most of the money Barney Bangam had hidden flew free — tens, twenties, fifties, hundreds. It was a green and bountiful rainfall of riches.

At last it came to an end.

"Tell me I'm not dreaming," Mrs. Andrews sighed. She had plopped down on the floor, awash in money.

Mrs. Aberdeen was clearly stunned. "I never really believed in the treasure." She held her hand over her throat as she gazed around the room. "Even when John Joseph Tranquil told us about it. Things like this just don't happen in the real world."

"Maybe that's because nobody has an uncle like Barney Bangam," Mr. Andrews said. "Listen, Mrs. Aberdeen," he went on practically. "Let's be sensible about this. The money should be gathered, counted, and sorted out, for starters."

It took a considerable time to do this, for every now and then someone would lose count and have to start over again. But, finally, the money was neatly stacked.

Charlie gave Mrs. Aberdeen a mischievous smile. "Are you going to put the money in your forget-me-not pillow?"

She laughed. "No, Charlie. Back it goes in the box. And then to the bank. I'm sure Uncle Barney knew that is exactly what I would do."

When they were in the car on their way to the bank, Tom nudged Ben. "I bet you read a lot of mysteries, don't you? The way you figured out the real clue was terrific."

"He doesn't have to read mysteries. Ben's a genius." Charlie leaned over the front seat and held out his hand to Ben. "Listen, Superkid, it's going to be a long year, so I'm going to have to learn to live with it. There are going to be plenty of days when I'll still hate your guts."

"And I'll hate yours," Ben reminded him.

Charlie agreed. "And you'll hate mine. But maybe, in between times, we can be friends. Want to shake on it?"

Ben's hand shot out promptly. "A half-time friend is better than no friend at all."

At the bank, John Joseph Tranquil welcomed the sight of the money as if it were a lost and willful puppy who had found his way home. He began to part Mrs. Aberdeen from the others with the skill of long practice.

"We must talk," he told her firmly. "There are investments to be made, perhaps a trust fund set up . . ."

"We'll just take off, then," Mr. Andrews said. He kissed Mrs. Aberdeen on both cheeks.

"I shall never forget your kindness," she told him gratefully. "All of you. So kind. Goodbye, dear boy." Mrs. Aberdeen pulled Ben close.

"I wonder if she'll remember about the wax

figures and the posters," Mr. Andrews wondered on the way home.

"She will." Charlie was certain. "She's that kind of a lady."

"We'll see," his father said.

And see they did, for one week later, Mrs. Aberdeen rang the Andrews's doorbell.

"I'm taking a flight back to Japan." She spoke so rapidly Charlie half expected the plane to be waiting out front on their driveway just so Mrs. Aberdeen could leap in and fly off. "Now, Mr. Andrews. I've made arrangements for all of the waxworks and the posters to be kept in storage until such time you have room for them in your store. Here's the ticket. I've paid in advance for delivery to your store as well. No, no, don't thank me," she went on in a rush. "I don't have much time for everything I still need to do. Now, boys," she turned to Charlie and Ben. "Oh, Tom, you're here, too. Good. I have a little surprise for you all. I have a cab waiting. Don't be concerned," she told Charlie's parents. "I'll send them home in the cab. Come with me, boys."

Though they were mystified, they followed her willingly. She would answer no questions, just repeated, "Wait and see."

Tom stared out the window. "Hey. This is the way to your Uncle Barney's house. Are we going there again?"

Mrs. Aberdeen smiled. "No, Tom. We're going to a place I'm sure you boys will enjoy."

When the cab finally stopped, Charlie shouted, "It's the Crosscreek Riding Stable. They're having a horse show, right? And you're taking us to see it!"

"Not exactly. Just pull up in front of the stable," Mrs. Aberdeen instructed the cab-driver.

When they stepped out of the cab, they were greeted by a small but sturdy man dressed in worn jeans and a dark T-shirt that advised *Get a Horse!* He led a chestnut mare whose mane gleamed in the sunlight and whose large brown eyes regarded the boys calmly.

"This is Bertha," the man told them.

"I wanted to thank you boys for all you did

for me," Mrs. Aberdeen explained. "And I wanted to give you a gift that would last, and one you could all share. I remembered that you boys said you had never been on a real horse. Well, Bertha is a real horse, and she's yours."

Mrs. Aberdeen beamed at the expressions of delight on the faces of all three boys.

"I've paid for riding lessons for the three of you for one full year. Mr. MacIntyre" — the man nodded when she mentioned his name — "will teach you to ride her, how to groom her, and whatever else you need to know."

Ben was thrilled, as were Tom and Charlie, but he was suddenly also doubtful. Up close, Bertha was huge.

"You want a lift up, just to see how it feels?" Mr. MacIntyre asked Ben.

Ben backed away. "I wouldn't know what to do."

"Don't worry," Mr. MacIntyre assured him. "You don't have to be a genius to ride a horse."

Ben looked at Charlie and Tom, then

grinned from ear to ear. The boys looked back at him with smiles that split their faces in two.

Mr. MacIntyre was puzzled. "Did I say something funny?"

The boys couldn't answer, for they were doubled over with laughter.

37901

j

Clifford, Eth

I hate your guts,
Ben Brooster

1395